Weekly Reader Children's Book Club presents

the Daddy Book

by Robert Stewart
Pictures by Don Madden

McGRAW-HILL BOOK COMPANY

A Division of McGraw-Hill Book Company
New York   St. Louis   San Francisco
Düsseldorf   London   Mexico   Sydney   Toronto

FOREWORD

I owe the idea for *The Daddy Book* to Robert Wing Stewart and Matthew Norton Stewart, who not only made me a daddy but introduced me to today's world of children's books. In reading and rereading dozens of them, I was taken by the fact that very few have daddies in them. Indeed there are many stories about "daddy ducks" and "daddy bears," but hardly any with "real live" daddies. It has also occurred to me that with more and more daddies spending more and more time with their children (and more mommies going to work), it might be fitting for daddies to have a book of their own, showing some of the things they do and some of the jobs they have. Perhaps daddies have been too mysterious to their children in the past, and maybe, in its own small way, *The Daddy Book* will dispel a bit of that—at least I'm certain it's one book I won't mind reading "one more time" before Robert and Matthew's lights go out.

R. S. S.

Stewart, Robert.
The daddy book.

SUMMARY : Describes the various activities of fathers at home and away.
1. Fathers—Fiction   I. Madden, Don. illus. II. Title.
PZ7 S8498Dad   [E]   72-000020
ISBN 0-07-061347-8
ISBN 0-07-061348-6 (lib. bdg.)

is for
Daddy,
who wears . . .

ties and bow ties

and socks:

long socks and

short socks,

dark socks

and

bright socks,

and trousers

and belts.

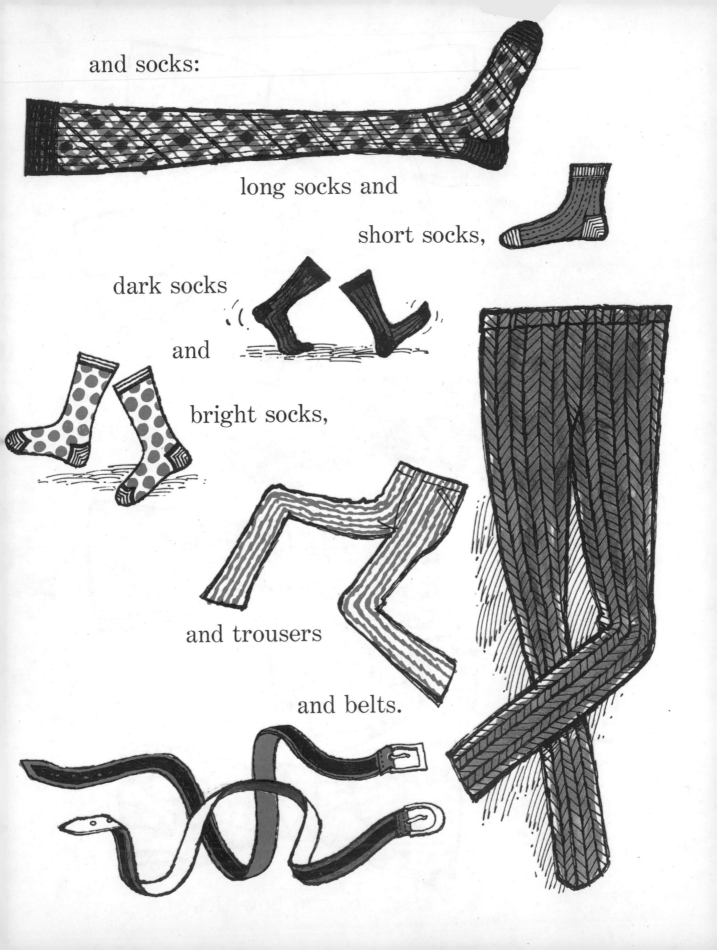

And daddies wear sweaters and mufflers
and hats and coats and raincoats and shoes:
lots of shoes and sneakers and boots.

Daddies have shirts of all kinds.

Some daddies are tall,

and some daddies are short.

Some daddies are thin,
and some daddies are fat.

Some daddies are white.
Some daddies are black.
Some daddies are red,
and some are yellow.

Some daddies
have
short hair,

and some daddies
have long hair,

and some daddies have  NO hair.

Some daddies
have beards, and
some daddies
have mustaches —

does yours?

Daddies have razors and razor blades,
and shaving cream and electric shavers,
and after-shave lotion and deodorant,
and combs and brushes and big towels,
and toothbrushes and toothpaste and soap.

Daddies have wrist watches

and wallets

and checkbooks

and briefcases

and attaché cases

and pens

and keys.

Some daddies have lawn mowers

and fishing rods

and tennis rackets

and golf clubs.

Some daddies wear glasses.

Some daddies smoke pipes.

A lot of daddies have cameras and projectors.

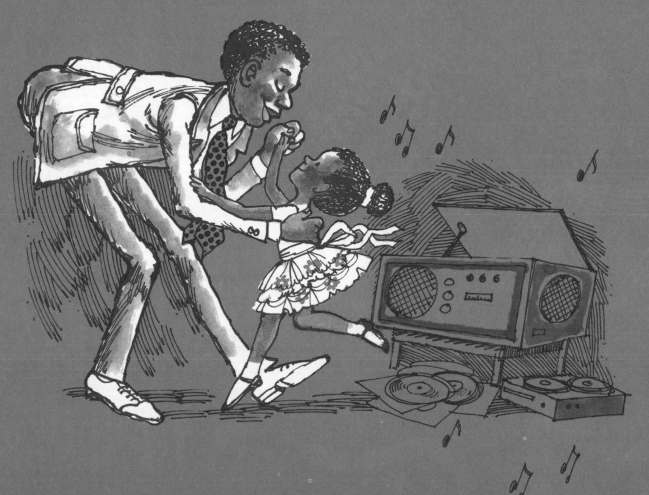

They have tape recorders
and record players
and radios.

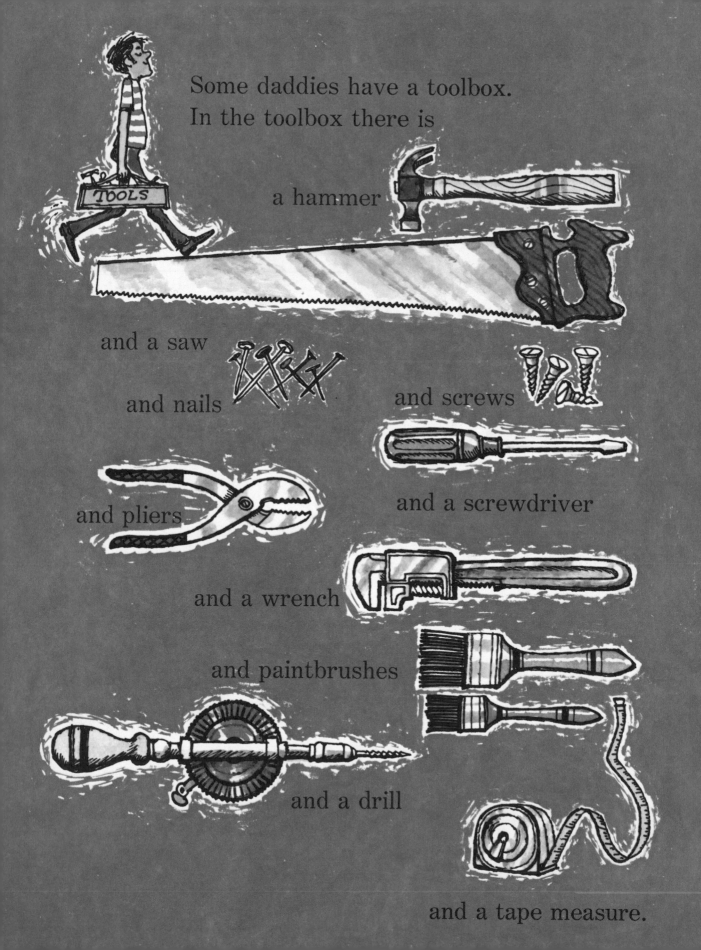

Some daddies have a toolbox.
In the toolbox there is

a hammer

and a saw

and nails

and screws

and a screwdriver

and pliers

and a wrench

and paintbrushes

and a drill

and a tape measure.

Daddy uses his tools
to hang curtains and pictures,
to paint walls and roofs,
to fix tables and chairs
and cribs and strollers

and toys and bicycles and tricycles.

Some daddies work in big buildings.
There are big elevators
and offices with desks,

and telephones
and typewriters
and adding machines
and filing cabinets.

Some daddies are doctors.

Some daddies are lawyers.

Some daddies are farmers.

Some daddies
are policemen

or firemen.

Some daddies drive buses.

Some daddies drive taxis
or subway trains
or trucks.

Some daddies are workmen who drive cranes or bulldozers with scoops.

ome daddies drive steamrollers or tractors.

What does your daddy do?

Is he an architect

artist

advertising man

actor

acrobat

businessman

boxer

carpenter

car salesman

dentist

director

electrician

engineer

hairdresser

handyman

ice-cream man

journalist

lab assistant

mechanic

musician

poet

painter

post-office worker

salesman

singer

scientist

script writer

technician

waiter

window cleaner

zoo keeper

When Daddy comes home from work
he brings the newspapers or toys
or groceries or something for Mommy.

Some daddies like to sit in a big chair
when they come home from work.
Some daddies like to eat a big dinner
or watch television.

Sometimes daddies play games
with their little boys or girls.
Does your daddy
help you build things
with blocks?

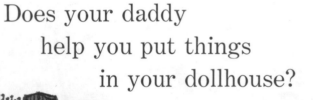

Does your daddy
help you put things
in your dollhouse?

Does your daddy help you sail boats in the bathtub?

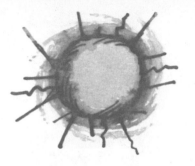

Does your daddy help you put
your racing tracks together?
Does he read you stories?
Pull you in your wagon?
Lift you on his shoulders?
Let you ride on his back?
Does he swing you in the air?

Where does Daddy take you when he has a day off?

For a ride in his car?

Or on a bus?

Or on the subway?

Does he take you in a taxi

or in a station wagon?

Or does Daddy
take you
on his bicycle?

Some daddies take their children to the zoo

or to the park

or to play baseball

or football.

Some daddies go skating

or skiing

or swimming

or boating.

Some daddies like to go on picnics. Does yours?
Does he buy you ice cream? Or popcorn? Or balloons?

Daddy often does what Mommy does.

He changes diapers.

Daddy cooks dinner

and washes dishes.

Does your daddy
give you a bath?

Put your pajamas on?

Put you to bed?

Sometimes daddies get angry.
Does your daddy ever tell you
to eat all your food?
Wash your hands?
Stay in your bed?
Pick up your toys?

But all daddies love
their little boys and girls.
No matter what.

Good
night,
Daddy!